Hamilton, Adams, and Co.

Verses for lent and easter tide

On suffering and the glory which shall follow

Hamilton, Adams, and Co.

Verses for lent and easter tide
On suffering and the glory which shall follow

ISBN/EAN: 9783741193484

Manufactured in Europe, USA, Canada, Australia, Japa

Cover: Foto ©Andreas Hilbeck / pixelio.de

Manufactured and distributed by brebook publishing software
(www.brebook.com)

Hamilton, Adams, and Co.

Verses for lent and easter tide

Lent and Easter-Tide.

Verses

for

Lent and Easter-Tide,

on

SUFFERING AND THE GLORY WHICH

SHALL FOLLOW.

By Thine Agony and bloody sweat,
By Thy Cross and Passion,
By Thy Precious Death and Burial,
By Thy glorious Resurrection and Ascension,
Good Lord, deliver us.

LONDON:
HAMILTON, ADAMS, AND Co., PATERNOSTER ROW.
SIDMOUTH:
THOMAS PERRY, FORE STREET.
1861.

Preface.

—◆—

A FEW words will be sufficient to account for the appearance of the following pages. Several of them were written to calm the sorrow, and relieve the loneliness of bereavement; and so they have become dear to the Writer's mind. To many sympathizing friends they will probably possess a like interest; and will serve to show the different moods and phases of sorrow and trust, of suffering and hope, under which, he thanks God, he has been disciplined.

Some of the verses have already appeared in different publications which are now out of print; these have been inserted as links to join the whole together in a Series for Lent and Easter.

It has long been a custom with the Writer to select "Verses" appropriate to the different "Church Seasons"; and to keep them as a kind of abiding thought for the Day. We all know how particular tunes, and certain poetical lines haunt the Memory, at first breaking in as a

PREFACE.

thought,—or under-current of thought,—on whatever we are doing, and whatever we are meditating, until at length they linger but as a faint echo; and then die away. Nevertheless they often leave some suggestion of peace, or some quieting influence behind them. This custom prompted the attempt to supply metrical thoughts, or aspirations for the use of those who would try the comfort and profit of such a practice.

Some may think that the beautiful "Thoughts in Verse" for the "Christian Year" have removed all necessity for any help beside them. But the weekly banquet of those "rich sweets," followed up uninterruptedly for many years, has still left some not so fastidious but that they can occasionally turn to other and simpler fare. The eager and still increasing taste for Poetry, devotional and suggestive, is a full proof of this. If this contribution, added to the stores which already exist, furnish one line which may suggest a new "holy thought" for a single day or hour, it will have answered some end, beside having supplied occupation to fill up an hour of loneliness, or to lead, into a better channel than repining, a mind temporarily unnerved by sorrow.

W. A. N.

Vicarage, Sidmouth,
  Lent, 1861.

Contents.

———

CONTENTS.

The Life of Jesus.

His Birth was one in no proud state arrayed,
Born in a stable, in a manger laid:
His Infancy in exiled flight was pass'd,
His Youth in toil and poverty and fast:

His Manhood's years Unrest and Travail fill,
His drink was tears, His meat His Father's Will:
In grief He lived, in bitterness He died,
Anguish'd in Soul, in Body crucified:

But now the Pathway of the Cross is o'er,
Pain, grief and anguish harass Him no more;
"The travail of His Soul" with joy He sees,—
Ten thousand times ten thousand victories.

Bear thou the Cross, seek not to lay it down,
After its burden comes the victor's Crown.

THE SHADOW OF THE CROSS.

Learner in Jesu's school, who in thy way
Seest dark lines thou canst not comprehend ;
Let not that shadow bring thy soul dismay,
Lo ! the bright distance where those dark lines end :
    It is the Shadow of the Cross,
      Along it Jesus trod ;
    Rest in its shade, keep in its path,
      It leads thee to thy God !

Pilgrim, who climbest up the rugged steep,
Struggling to leave earth's misty vale behind ;
But treadest timidly, as shadows deep
Cross ev'ry turn as up thy footsteps wind :
    It is the Shadow of the Cross,
      Let not thy footsteps roam ;
    Keep in its shade, though it be dark,
      It leads thee to thy home !

Repentant one, that carriest within
A load of pain and the sad signs of woe,—
The heavy burden of remember'd sin,—
And a dark grief which sinks thy spirit low :
    It is the Shadow of the Cross,
      Stay 'neath its shadow, stay ;
    It leads thee to the fount, whose stream
      Can wash thy guilt away !

Mourner, who sittest watching by the Tomb,
Weaving fond chaplets for the sacred dead ;
And seest, through thy tears, a line of gloom,
Resting in shadow on that narrow bed :
    It is the Shadow of the Cross,
      Whose hidden side is bright ;
    Above it see yon starry Crown,
      Yon beams of endless light !

Litany for Lent.

"If thou canst not, with S. John, contemplate divine and lofty things, thou canst cast thyself, with Mary Magdalene, at Christ's feet, and with broken spirit and contrite heart, seek the forgiveness of thy sins, where-with thou hast so often offended Him."

In mercy, Lord, draw near,
My heart, my soul, my thought, my ev'ry sense,
I fain would bend in lowly penitence,
Good Lord, in mercy hear!

Prostrate before Thee laid,
I breathe from wounded breast my sad lament;
In broken sobs my anguish'd sighs are sent,
Good Lord, be near to aid!

My thoughts within me burn
My heart is parch'd and pines with with'ring grief,
Nor can my scalding tears impart relief,
Good Lord, in mercy turn!

Guilt on my spirit weighs—
A load too heavy is my sin to bear,—
I sink beneath it,—Lord, in mercy spare,
Good Lord, be near to raise!

O hear a troubled heart;
Its broken accents and its burden'd sighs
I know Thy pitying ear will not despise,
Good Lord, Thy help impart!

My downcast soul release,
Pour in Thy balm, Thy blood, Thy healing grace;
Come, cleanse my heart, make it Thy resting-place,
    Come, Lord, and whisper peace!

O cleanse it from all guile,
Wash me, till white as snow my sin appears;
And in the place of dark and dismal fears,
    Good Lord, vouchsafe Thy smile!

Thy gracious pardon send,
O let my sin-bound soul rejoice again,
Breathe Thy absolving love,—remove my chain,
    Good Lord, in mercy bend!

Empty my soul appears,
No gift, no sacrifice have I to bring,—
Save tears,—a broken heart's sad offering,
    Good Lord, accept my tears!

And as my footsteps go
From stage to stage through Sorrow's Baca-vale,
Let not Thy wells of healing comfort fail,
    Good Lord, Thy strength bestow!

When I draw near the grave,
And down the Vale of Death my soul must glide,—
O let me feel Thy presence by my side,
    Good Lord, be near to save!

And when that hour shall be
That all who sleep in dust Thy voice shall hear,
And at Thy strict tribunal must appear,
    Good Lord, remember me!

Rest in Jesus.

"O that I had wings like a dove, for then would I flee away, and be at rest." PSALM lv. 6.

Why, my soul, cast down and weary,
    Pinest thou for wings to flee!
Each new place would still seem dreary,
    Change would bring no peace to thee:
Seek thy home in JESU's breast,
Thither flee, and be at rest!

JESUS is a rock to hide thee,
    JESUS is thy sheltering ark;
Safe in His recesses bide thee,
    While the sky is wild and dark:
Frayed with fear, with grief oppress'd,
Flee to HIM, and be at rest!

Art thou bruised? His hand can bind thee;
    Stained? His Blood can cleanse each sin;
Art thou lost? His love can find thee;
    Outcast? He can let thee in:
Make His deepest love thy nest,
Flee to HIM, and be at rest!

Dost thou mourn for friends departed,
    Dear and loved ones passed away?
Art thou hopeless? broken-hearted?
    JESUS is the mourner's stay:
He uplifts the sore-distrest,
Flee to HIM, and be at rest!

V.

Future fears, do they oppress thee?
Shrinkest thou from coming shame?
Fears may fright thee, doubts distress thee,
Jesus will be still the same:
Near to plead thy sad request,
Flee to HIM, and be at rest!

Jesu, Jesu, hear my sighing,
Smitten is my heart with grief;
Knocking at Thy gate and crying,
Open, Lord, and give relief:—
To Thy sacred, shelt'ring breast,
Lord, I flee, and find my rest!

"Above all things and in all things, O my soul, thou shalt rest in the Lord alway, for He Himself is the everlasting Rest of the Saints.

"Grant me, O most sweet and loving Jesus, to rest in Thee above all creatures, above all health and beauty, above all glory and honour, above all power and dignity, ... above all things visible and invisible, and above all that Thou art not, O my God.

"For surely my heart cannot truly rest, nor be entirely contented, unless it rest in Thee, and surmount all gifts and all creatures whatsoever.

"O when shall it be granted to me, to consider in quietness of mind and see how sweet Thou art, my Lord God!

"When shall I fully gather up myself to Thee, that by reason of my love to Thee, I may not feel myself, but Thee alone!

"Many evils occur in this vale of miseries which do often trouble, grieve and overcloud me; often hinder and distract me, allure and entangle me, so that I can have no free access unto Thee, nor enjoy the sweet welcomings which are ever ready for the blessed spirits.

"I will not hold my peace, nor cease to pray, until Thy grace return again, and Thou speak inwardly unto me."

THOMAS A KEMPIS' *Imitation of Christ.*

It is done.

Rev. xxi. 6.

❖

"It is done!"—
I heard a great and mighty voice revealing:
  Out from God's throne issued the solemn sound;
Through the wide air, o'er the deep ocean pealing,
    I heard the voice rebound:
The Heav'ns rejoiced throughout their happy dwell-
    Hell writhed in keener pain;   [ings;
And Death and dark Corruption at its knellings
    Recoiled in fright throughout their charnel-reign:
Angel hosannas hailed it in their song,
Dreary with doom earth's rocks it roll'd among,
And the dim phantom realms whisper'd in echoes long—
      "It is done!"

"It is done!"
Fell on my ear as the old year was dying,
    And its last knell startled the midnight's sleep:
And cycles past to the drear sound replying,
      Answered in murmurs deep:—
"Come, link of ages, come, thy compeers call thee,
      Years which like thee have fled;
Bring thy recording scroll, though it appal thee,
      With mercies wasted, and with moments sped:
In vain for thee the aching eye shall turn;
In vain for thee repenting hearts shall burn;
No more, ah! never more, shalt thou to them return—
      "It is done!"

"It is done!"

I heard this utter'd o'er a soul departing:
  A pallid form in death before me lay,
And sobs of anguish from rent bosoms starting,
  Called me to pause and pray.
A life, with all its weight of life, was ended,
  Eye, speech, pulse, heart were dumb;
A Soul up to its Source had re-ascended,
  A mortal man Immortal had become.
No wealth of worlds could buy a moment more;
No tears, no treaties could that life restore,
Death mutter'd, as it closed the vast, eternal door—
    "IT IS DONE!"

"It is done!"

I heard an angel's mighty trumpet sounding:
  One foot on earth he fixed,—one on the sea;
Thunders and voices in deep notes redounding,
  Rolled long and awfully:
His hand he lifted with majestic motion
  High up to heav'n;—and swore
By HIM who made the sky and earth and ocean,
  That Time with all its works should be no more.
The Sun and Moon fell from the flaming pole!
The shrivell'd skies were folded as a scroll!
And o'er the world's wide wreck, I heard the thunders
    "IT IS DONE!"   [roll—

"It is done!"

I saw a form in awful brightness seated,—
   A King and Judge,—upon a great white Throne:
Angels, archangels, loud His Name repeated;
   And far His glory shone :.
Before that Throne all who had lived assembled,
   A countless multitude ;—
Before that Throne the cow'ring guilty trembled ;
   Before that Throne the righteous fearless stood :
To all that host God's justice was revealed,
To all that host a changeless doom was sealed,
And round the great white Throne the rolling sentence
   "IT IS DONE!"   [pealed—

"It is done!"   [der,

Man heed these words! Their solemn meaning pon-
   Read, mark, learn, write them, fix them in thy
They may recall thy footsteps if thou wander; [soul :
   They may thy path control.
Thy days, unknown to thee, by God are numbered—
   Small may their number be,—
If in a dream of shadows thou hast slumbered,
   Awake, arouse thee, heed thy life, and flee !
Another warning Season cries "prepare ; "
Soon shall Life's vision melt into thin air,
And solemn anxious whispers at thy death declare—
   "IT IS DONE!"

Go thou, and sin no more!

Go thou, and sin no more! For know, thy guilt
Bruised with its load the sad Redeemer's soul;
To cleanse thy sin His sacred blood was spilt,
Thy stripes He bore,—His stripes can make thee whole.
Oh shall His pangs, His Blood, His Death be vain!
Wilt thou despise His love, His tender call!
He hath redeem'd thee, bought thee by His pain;
His help is near, to raise thee if thou fall.
                    Go thou, and sin no more!

Sin not in *thought!* For He thy thoughts can see,
And calls them oft to dwell on Him alone!
Sin not in *word!* thy words shall follow thee,
And speak again before God's awful throne!
Sin not in *deed!* for deeds can never die,
They live to tell our pardon or despair;
Thought, word, and deed unto the judgment fly,
Going before us, to await us there!
                    Go thou, and sin no more!

Deep is the peace the pardon'd conscience knows;
Blessed the witness God's free Spirit gives;
Sweet the Communion which from JESUS flows;
Holy the Trust which on His promise lives.
Oh seek this Peace! Christ's own, Christ's hallow'd
Be still, and listen for God's voice within;   [Peace!
Faith shall from fear thy struggling soul release,
And heav'nly healing stay the wounds of sin:—
                    Go thou, and sin no more!

x.

Eternity.

Translated from the German of DANIEL WÜLFFER, 1650.

Eternity, Eternity,
How long art thou Eternity !
And yet our years how swift in flight,—
Fleet as the war-horse to the fight,—
As post ; or ship ; or bird on wing ;
Or arrow from the bowman's string.
    O mortal, heed Eternity !

Eternity, Eternity,
How long art thou Eternity !
As a sphere's circles wide extend,
With no beginning and no end :
Thus, O Eternity, with thee
No entrance and no end can be.
    O mortal, heed Eternity !

Eternity, Eternity,
How long art thou Eternity !
A ring thou art, whose outmost bound
No tongue can tell, no thought can sound ;
Thy centre ALWAYS—ever nigh,—
And NEVER thine extremity.
    O mortal, heed Eternity !

Eternity, Eternity,
How long art thou Eternity !
Should in its flight a bird appear
And take one grain, each thousandth year,
From all the sand of hill and sea
Till all had gone,—thou still would'st be !
    O mortal, heed Eternity !

Eternity, Eternity,
How long art thou Eternity !
He who, once poor, earth's pathway trod,
Shall rest for ever rich in God ;
There near the Highest, love and bless
In ecstasy of happiness.
O mortal, heed Eternity !

Eternity, Eternity,
How long art thou Eternity !
Here for a moment joys may flow,
In thee we enter endless woe ;
Here for a moment griefs annoy,
In thee we enter endless joy.
O mortal, heed Eternity !

Eternity, Eternity,
How long art thou Eternity !
Thus speaks to God who thinks of Thee,
"Here try, here judge, here punish me ;
"Now let not Thy strict justice spare,
"But when this life is past, forbear."
O mortal, heed Eternity !

Eternity, Eternity,
How long art thou Eternity !
"I speak,—Eternity,—do thou,
"Be wise, O man, and heed me *now* ;
"For I shall be the sinner's pain,
"And I the good man's endless gain.
O mortal, heed Eternity !"

Eternity, Eternity,
How long art thou Eternity !
As long as God Himself shall be,
So long shall last Hell's agony ;—
So long shall glory's bliss remain ;—
Oh endless bliss ! Oh endless pain !
O mortal, heed Eternity !

A Prayer.

Before the silver cord be loosed,*
Or the golden bowl be broken,
And the wheel run down at the cistern,
And the pitcher
Of all the tribes of mankind
Be broken at the fountain ;   [great !
Have mercy upon me, O God , for Thy mercies are

Before the dust
Shall return to the earth,
And we become but ashes ;
And our bodies
Once so beautiful and wonderful,
Shall be turned to corruption ;   [great !
Have mercy upon me, O God, for Thy mercies are

Before the with'ring breath
Of Death shall smite us,
As trees are smitten by a blast ;
And our bodies put forth
Diseases, like sad heralds, telling
The end of Life is near ;   [great !
Have mercy upon us, O God, for Thy mercies are

* Ecclesiastes xii. 6.

EPHREM SYRUS.

Joy in Heaven.

"Joy in heaven! joy in heaven!
O'er a penitent forgiven!"
Tell it to the contrite heart,
Aching with its rankling smart;
Tell it to the burden'd breast,
Sinking, languishing for rest;
Tell it to the suppliant, bent
Low to earth and penitent,—
   There is joy o'er him in heaven!

"Joy in heaven! joy in heaven!
O'er a penitent forgiven!"
Tell it to the sad, who wait
At the Saviour's mercy-gate;
Bowed with sin, and pierced with grief,
Craving pardon, and relief;
Tell them in their pain and fear,
Jesus bends a pitying ear,—
   There is joy o'er them in heaven!

"Joy in heaven! joy in heaven!
O'er a penitent forgiven!"
Tell it to each outcast son,
Who his course of shame hath run,
But whose better feelings roam,
Backward to his Father's home;—
Tell him as his form is prest
Closely to His Father's breast,—
   There is joy o'er him in heaven!

Spirit of Prayer.

What is this longing? what this struggling feeling
  Unstill'd, unsatisfied, by earthly din?
This heart's unrest! this spirit-cry revealing
        Deep wants within?
What are these promptings, like soft notes upbraiding
        The soul's despair?—
Is it God's Presence mortal weakness aiding,
        Spirit of Prayer?

What is this rapture? what these seraph pinions
  Whose soarings waft me far above the skies?
What this bright vision? spreading Heav'n's dominions
        Before mine eyes?
What impulse draws my inward sight, up-gazing
        Through the bright air?
Is it God's love this earthly spirit raising,
        Spirit of Prayer?

What are these sounds beyond all mortal utt'ring,—
  Eloquent breathings, supplications deep,—
Sweet Heav'n-wing'd words, floating like angels flutt'r-
        O'er a Saint's sleep?   [ing
Is this the voice of fervent prayer ascending
        Heav'n's shining stair?
Is this the sound to which God's ear is bending,
        Spirit of Prayer?

XV.

What is that voice that softly intercedeth?
    What that sweet incense filling all around?
What that dear merit which more loudly pleadeth
                    Than mightiest sound?
What is that pow'r which Heav'n's shut portal shaketh,
                    And ent'reth there?
Is that the Intercession JESUS maketh,
                    Spirit of Prayer?

Oh! what is this sweet quiet gently spreading?
    This spirit's calm, in which my soul is bound
What this hush'd awe, as if the foot were treading
                    On holy ground?
What is this Peace, like earth's and Heav'n's union,
                    When skies are fair?
Is this the stillness of the Saint's Communion,
                    Spirit of Prayer?

What is this aid which gives me such resistance
    To strive, to run, to wrestle for the Crown?
What this kind hand which lends me such assistance,
                    When beaten down?
What is this unseen aid which me sustaineth
                    With ready care?
Is this the strength my poor petition gaineth,
                    Spirit of Prayer?

Oh! then may I for ever give my being,
    My soul, my life, as long as life shall be,
To Thy sweet praise; and be for ever fleeing,
                    My God to Thee.
Oh! may my heart ever with rapt emotion
                    To THEE repair;
And lose itself in Thy intense devotion,
                    Spirit of Prayer!

Hosanna to the King.

FOR PALM SUNDAY.

"On the next day much people that were come to the feast, when they heard that Jesus was coming to Jerusalem, took branches of palm-trees, and went forth to meet Him, and cried, Hosanna! Blessed is the King of Israel that cometh in the name of the Lord." S. JOHN xii. 12, 13.

"And when He was come near, He beheld the city, and wept over it." S. LUKE xix. 41.

What king draws near? whose coming fills
    The air with such acclaim?
Who rides in triumph from yon hills?
    Whose is that echoed Name?
In eager joy adown that steep,
Still on, the waving palm-boughs sweep,
    Still far those voices ring;
      From side to side
      They answer wide,
          "Hosanna to the King!"

The tow'rs of proud Jerusalem
    Shone from their lofty height;
Her Temple, like a lustrous gem,
    Blazed in the morning's light:
On to her gates the shouting throng,
Strewing their garments, move along,
    And still in triumph sing,—
      Through Kedron's ford
      In rapt accord,—
          "Hosanna to the King."

But why amid that scene of light,
    That triumph down the steep,—
Gazing on yonder city's height,
    Did JESUS pause and weep?

What vision did His eye discern,
That triumph into grief to turn,
　To tears that welcoming ?—
　　As from the crowd
　　There burst aloud,
　　　　　"Hosanna to the King."

Ah well He knew that soon that cry
　In other notes would rise ;
That shout be changed to mockery,
　To hate those ecstasies :
He knew that, fickle as the breeze,
Another mood that crowd would seize,
　Another echo ring :—
　　"Away with Him"
　　Would change that Hymn
　　　　　"Hosanna to the King."

He saw that Temple, Zion's pride,
　In ruins scattered round,
Those stately tow'rs on every side
　Laid level with the ground :
And Judah's children sad and lorn,
Wasted, and parched, and famine-worn,
　Scatter'd and wandering :—
　　This changed to wail
　　That cry of 'hail,'
　　　　　"Hosanna to the King : "

Oh ! sacred tears which JESUS shed,
　There in that triumph-scene !
Oh ! sacred sympathy which bled
　O'er human sorrows keen !
Oh ! sacred Pity which still flows
O'er human sadness, human woes,
　Its healing balm to bring !—
　　All still are nigh
　　Where bruised hearts sigh,
　　　　　"Hosanna to the King ! "

The last days of Jesus.

" In the day time He was teaching in the Temple; and at night He went out and abode in the mount that is called the Mount of Olives." S. LUKE xxi. 37.

DAY IN THE TEMPLE! Thither JESUS went
  Morning by morning, long ere hour of prayer;
Within its courts, each live-long day He spent,
  Teaching the eager crowds that gather'd there:
Go daily to God's House; in faith draw near,
To meet your God,—your Saviour's voice to hear!

Oh! to have heard His very words descend,
  Like gentle dew, charming the heart from pain;
Bidding the broken reed no longer bend,
  Bidding the smoking flax to burn again:
Oh! to have heard the guilty soul's release
From those absolving words, " depart in peace!"

Oh! to have seen those miracles which gave
  Sight to the blind, and healing to the weak;
Which called the dead to rise from out the grave,
  The deaf to hear,—the silent tongue to speak:
Oh! to have touched with timid hand, but sure,
That garment's hem, and felt its virtue cure.

Yet vain the wish, and faithless the request:—
  Christ still is present, still in pow'r is near,
Near to each soul which seeks Him as its rest,
  Near to revive it, and its prayer to hear:
Daily He waits to bless, to teach, to heal,
Where the hush'd few within His Temple kneel!

xix.

NIGHT ON THE MOUNTAIN! JESUS oft withdrew
  From the throng'd scene, to breathe the calmer air;
The mountain side His sacred vigils knew,
  His silent solitude and midnight prayer:
Strength'ning His firm resolve, and learning still,
Deeper submission to His Father's Will.

There oft in still communion, calm and lone,
  Whole nights He passed on saintly Olivet,
'Neath the cold moon which on His watchings shone,
  While with chill dew His down-bent head was wet:
Oh! who can know each sacred, struggling word
Which that awed Mount, those hours of midnight hear

And wilt not thou, my soul, like JESUS seek
  The silent hour, the midnight musing still?
Wilt thou not oft in holy accents speak
  With Him on calm Seclusion's sacred hill?
Shall not the Saviour hear thy earnest tone,
Heard in awed silence, heard by Him alone?

Oh! talk with Him; He bends a list'ning ear,
  He knows thy thoughts, He tells thy struggling sighs;
He who oft prayed, to help thy prayer is near,
  He who can pity, bids thy prayer arise!
If JESUS nightly watched, if JESUS prayed—
Oh! can thy watch, thy eager prayer be stayed!

xx.

The Anointing of Jesus.

FOR TUESDAY IN PASSION WEEK.

"Let her alone: against the day of My burying hath she kept this." S. JOHN xii. 7.

That precious ointment sold !
That costly spikenard with its odor sweet !
   That gift, worth more than gold,
That flowed in grateful tribute on thy feet,
Telling emotions deep and manifold !

What price for love so rare !
That poured its all on that dear form divine !
   What price with hers compare,
Who gave her tears to wash those feet of thine,
And wiped them with the napkin of her hair !

Angels that gift might take,
And lay it at the footstool of God's throne ;
   That its rich worth might make
Memorial of her, not on earth alone,
But in Thy Father's presence, for *Thy* Sake !

Against Thy burying
That sweetest ointment was so richly stored ;
   Her secret love could bring,
In its devoted forethought for her Lord,
No living gift, no common offering.

O that such costly love
Could in my heart such full devotion stir,
   And each deep impulse move ;
That I, in one self-sacrifice, like her
Could with one outpour'd gift my ardor prove.

What can my heart present ?
Which Thou, O dearest Lord, wilt not despise,
　　What love ? What lavishment
Of sweetest frankincense ? What sacrifice ?
What flowing tears ? What heart with sorrow rent ?

　　If I could bring the store
Of richest treasures and of spices sweet :
　　If I could rivers pour
Of oil, and fragrant unguents on Thy feet ;—
They could no pardon gain ! no peace restore !

　　Tears, Lord, from streaming eyes,
Deep scalding tears of hidden grief I bring,
　　Remorse and struggling sighs,
And painful sobs with stifled uttering,—
This is my gift, my lowly sacrifice.

　　A broken contrite heart
This too beneath Thy bitter Cross I lay,
　　Bleeding with many a smart,
Trembling with fear and horrible dismay,
To think how cold I am,—how kind Thou art !

　　Though at Thy mercy gate
Prostrate in soul, in sorrow penitent,
　　In watch and prayer I wait,
With spirit sorely bruised, and body bent,
Can this for guilt's transgression compensate ?

　　Ah ! No ! no tear, no groan,
No contrite heart, no form in lowest dust
　　Can for one sin atone ;
In Thy dear ransom is my only trust,
My Hope, my Peace, my Life art Thou alone.

xxii.

The bitter cup of Jesus.

FOR WEDNESDAY IN PASSION WEEK.

" He shall drink of the brook in the way." Psalm cx. 7.

Dark was the brook which Jesus bowed to drink,
  Bitter the cup He quaffed,
  A life-long bitterness :—
Yet no o'erwhelming flood, no cruel draught,
  No weight of grief, no sore distress,
    Could make His spirit shrink :
He drained the cup, He drank the bitter stream,
Our cup to sweeten, and our souls redeem.

In flight and toil, from Childhood's early years,
  He knew each trying scene
  Of human poverty ;
In fastings often, and in hunger keen,
  His meat was sorrow's burdened sigh,
    His cup was one of tears :
Faint with fatigue, drooping with weary tread,
The Saviour had not where to lay His head.

By the drear heart, beside the couch of pain,
  Oft was His presence nigh ;
  Grieving with those that grieved,
His gentle love and touching sympathy
  The mourner's trembling heart relieved,
    The sick made whole again :
And whilst His pity bade *them* not to weep,
He drank their draught of sadness large and deep.

xxiii.

To many a Marah stream His footsteps turned,
    To sad Bethesda's pool,
    To Nain's crowded gate;
But as He held the healing draught to cool
    Sharp Pain, to cheer the desolate,
        And comfort those who mourned,
His soul was drinking low at sorrow's spring,
For wounded hearts and human suffering.

Through Kedron's brook He tasted by the way
    Of dreariness and dole;
    In lone Gethsemane
Billow on billow broke upon His soul,
    While wrestling in His agony
        Along the ground He lay:
In sharpest woe the awful Cup He drained,
And all alone our crushing Guilt sustained!

O drink, my soul, drink of Thy Saviour's woe;
    The painful pathway tread,
    Which He in grief once trod:
Weep that for thee His tortured Body bled;
    Weep that for thee thy Lord and God
        Such pangs should undergo:
Trace, day by day, with shame and anguish sore,
The cruel Passion which for thee He bore.

Follow His steps: His Cross take up and bear
    Along the Bitter Way,
    With penitential sigh:
Watch with thy Lord, in awful wrestlings pray;
    Each wrong wish curb and crucify,
        No self-denial spare:
Stand by His Cross, there all His sorrow see,
Dark was the brook which Jesus drank for thee.

xxiv.

The Agony of Jesus.

FOR THURSDAY IN PASSION WEEK.

" Could ye not watch with Me one hour ?"   MATT. xxvi. 40.

Canst thou not watch one hour ?
Thee have I watched in deepest love as mine,
  Since,—like a tender flower,
    As yet unstain'd within
    By any wilful sin,—
Thou didst receive my grace, and solemn sign :
From thy first years my love has watched by thee,
  Canst thou not watch with ME ?

  Thee have I watched, when thought
First ripen'd into act ; and thy new shame
  Blush'd at Guilt's faintest blot ;
    O'er thee My love has bent,
    While, yet impenitent,
Thy untold sin has burnt with smother'd flame :
To pardon and give peace I watched for thee,
  Canst thou not watch with ME ?

  Thee I have watched, when snares,
Invisible, like covered pitfalls, lay
  To catch thee unawares ;
    Then I thy steps have held,
    And the dark wile dispell'd
And moved the subtle danger from thy way :
Lest thou shouldst fall, oft I have watched for thee,
  Canst thou not watch with ME ?

I, too, have watched thee there,
Where My good angels camp'd thy path around;
    And kept thee in their care,
        Cheering thy hour of grief
        And minist'ring relief,
Raising thy fainting courage from the ground:
In all their watchings I have watched for thee,
    Canst thou not watch with ME?

Through the still night in prayer
Oft I have wrestled, oft for thee have cried;
    For thee the Cross I bare,
        In hunger and unrest,
        With inward pangs opprest,
In unseen anguish, each day crucified:
In awful vigils I have watched for thee,
    Canst thou not watch with ME?

Thee I have watched; and wept
Sad tears above thy fall, thy shame, thy guilt,
    While thou hast heedless slept:
        A stricken man of woes,
        With sorrow's bitter throes
Goading My heart, till all its blood was spilt,
I have in agony oft watched for thee:
    Canst thou not watch with ME?

Canst thou not watch one hour?
One hour in love, for ME who loved thee so;
    Has not My Sorrow power
        To pierce thy yielding heart,
        And bid its anguish smart
At My unutter'd grief, My bitter woe:
Crush'd 'neath thy load of sin I watched for thee,
    Canst thou not watch with ME?

xxvi.

The sufferings of Jesus.

FOR GOOD FRIDAY.

"Is it nothing to you, all ye that pass by ! Behold and see if there be any sorrow like to my sorrow ?" LAM. i. 12.
"The chastisement of our peace was upon Him." ISAIAH liii. 5.

JESUS, my suffering Lord,
Weeping repentant tears I gaze on Thee ;
One dying look down from Thy Cross accord,
　　　Saviour, to me.
No agony was ever like to Thine,
　JESUS, my Lord and God ;
No victim less submissive, less divine,
　　　Could bear that rod,
Or tread the tear-wash'd path which Thou hast trod !

　What flame is this that scars
Thine inmost breast and wrings Thine heart with pain ?
What large red drops are these,—these sad soul-tears,
　　　Which fall like rain ?
Was such the untold stress, and strain so great
　Of Thy soul's agony,
From sin's dread curse, and sorrow's crushing weight
　　　Our souls to free ;
And let our wearied spirits rest in Thee !

　What means that traitor kiss ?
That faithless band, thus timidly that flies ?
What coward tongue, what daring oath is this,
　　　Which Thee denies ?
Is it, dear Lord,—forsaken ones that Thou
　Shouldst as Thy friends proclaim ;
And on each contrite heart and ransom'd brow
　　　Write Thy new Name,
Giving them faith for fear, and joy for shame !

xxvii.

Why to that judgment-seat
Art Thou, like plaintless lamb, thus meekly led?
What ruthless hands, what impious smitings, beat
That low-bent head?
Is this meek Lamb,—is this dread Judge,—that we
Yet unaccused may stand,—
Healed through Thy cruel stripes and cleansed by
A spotless band,   [Thee,
Bright with Thy glory,—blest at Thy right hand!

Why does that knotted scourge
Plough its deep furrows on Thy back all sore?
Why does each thong, tearing Thy dear flesh, urge
Blood from each pore?
Is it that Love, staying the chast'ning rod
With mercy's gentle arm,
May to our souls, smitten and bruised of God,
Bring healing balm;
Changing the earthly rod to heav'nly palm!

Why is that crown of thorn
Piercing Thy brow with sharp and bitter throes?
Why are those temples,—marr'd with torture,—torn
Till the blood flows?
Is it that we on peaceful brows may wear
Celestial diadems;
Crown'd kings by Thee, with shining crowns, all fair
With sparkling gems,—
Crowns far excelling regal anadems!

Why is that robe of show
Put on in scorn,—purple and tarnish'd gold,—
While ah! sad contrast! the pale "man of woe"
Mock'd we behold?
Is it that robes, glist'ning with radiant light,
May on Thy ransom'd shine?
Robes wash'd from sin and stain,—and made most
With blood of Thine,—   [white
Robes which the Righteous wear,—vesture divine!

Why is that Body rack'd,
Distended,—tortured,—writhing there in pain ?
Why is each bone displaced, each fibre crack'd
      With the sharp strain ?
Why on that Cross raised from the earth on high,
  Dost Thou for us atone ?
Why from Thy altar bursts that Passion-cry,
      That piercing groan ?
Is that dread Cross our pathway to Thy throne !

  Why do those pins impale
To that rough wood those tender hands of Thine,
Why rends each numbing stroke, each griding nail
      Those feet divine ?
Is it that we our up-stretch'd hands may raise
  To Thy kind Mercy-seat,
And in the foot-track of Thy holy ways
      Hasten our feet,
Till made by Thee,—for Thy blest presence meet !

  Why is that taunting reed
Raised to Thy parching lips, with bitter gall ?
Can dying thirst such cruel mock'ry need ?
      Or that sad call ?
Was this Thy thirst, that we may quaff the cup
  From the eternal streams
Out of God's throne, fill'd by bright angels up ;
      All earthly themes
Lost in oblivious draughts of heav'nly dreams !

  Why does that glitt'ring spear
Pierce the warm fount of that unthrobbing heart ?
Why from that deep-gash'd side does water clear,
      And red blood start ?
Is it that through the torn and tortur'd veil
  Of that side keenly riv'n,
We may Redemption's open passage hail,
      And access given
By that new, living way to enter Heav'n !

Why is that night-black shroud
Over Creation's face at mid-day spread!
Why at that cry, the last,—and yet so loud,—
      Droops down Thy head?
Old Death himself is overcome by death,
  Spoiled are his victories;
The Lord of Life and Death him vanquisheth
      There as He dies,
And the Grave's gate unbarr'd, wide open flies!

Why in yon chilly tomb
Lay they, in linen folds, that corse so pale?
Shall that still silence, and that dreary gloom
      Ever prevail?
No! no! that guard-watch'd stone and sepulchre
  Thrown down at morning's light,—
And angel-forms, seen in those chambers drear,
      In dazzling white,
Shall tell the Lord of Life rises in might!

Bearing Thy Cross, dear Lord,
Thee may we follow, meek and lowly here;
Oh! let Thy gracious hand its aid afford,
      And catch each tear.
Then may we quit the Cross, and follow Thee
  Up where Thy glories shine;
And in Thy radiant Presence ever be,
      Welcomed as Thine,
Blest with the Blessed hosts, Saviour Divine!

"Nothing is more efficacious to cure the wounds of conscience than an earnest meditation on the wounds of Christ."

                S. BERNARD.

"O unspeakable and boundless goodness of God, who hath vouchsafed so many and so great blessings to mankind through the Cross of Jesus. Glory, worship, and power be unto Thy Goodness for ever."

                EPHREM SYRUS.

✠ ✠
✠

The two Maries.

FOR EASTER EVEN.

"And there was Mary Magdalene, and the other Mary, sitting over against the sepulchre." S. MATT. xxvii. 61.

How hush'd the scene! How peaceful the repose,
The breathless awe, the silence all around!
What soft, unearthly ray the moonlight throws!
The air how still! That stillness how profound!
No foot is heard, save the slow sentry's tread,
Stirs not the palm's tall fan,—the olive's leaf,
A sabbath quiet round that Tomb is shed,
The Maries weep, but weep in voiceless grief:
Ye two, who sit, like marble mourners, near
With veiléd heads bent sadly on the breast;
There's solemn homage in your silent tear,—
No wail, no sigh,—for JESUS *is at rest!*

That Tomb in Joseph's garden conquers fear,
Peaceful as that, the hallow'd dead repose;
No din of earth, no troubled sound they hear,
The sacred Cross its shadow o'er them throws.
Those two who watch, with anguish'd, hidden smart,—
Those tears which flow so silent to the dust,—
Are but an emblem of the grieving heart,
Whose woe is mute, whose waiting—holy trust:
Our dear ones are with JESUS; wherefore weep?
No toil their limbs, no griefs their hearts molest;
How still their sleeping-place! how calm their sleep!
Break not their hush'd repose,—*they are at rest!*

xxxi.

THE

Cross and Tomb of Jesus.

FOR EASTER EVEN.

" O death, where is thy sting? O grave, where is thy victory."
1 Cor. xv. 55.

Bow'd with sorrow, bruised with sin,
Sad and bleeding heart draw near ;
Scared without and faint within,
Come and seek thy shelter here.
Dost thou weep ? Thy Saviour shed
Tears of sorrow, tears of blood :
Art thou wounded ? JESUS bled,
Bled for thee a healing flood :
Art thou burden'd ? JESUS bore
All thy weight of sin and woe :
Weeping, wounded, burden'd, sore,
Grief like His thou canst not know :
Cease thy weeping : come and see
All thy Saviour bore for thee :
Come and lay thy grief aside,
At the Cross where JESUS died.

Weary heart, oppress'd with fear,
Feeble one whom pains consume,
Come and find your shelter here,
Come and watch by JESU's tomb :
Must thou sleep ? thy Saviour lay
In death's calm and silent sleep :
Must thy spirit pass away ?
JESUS lives thy soul to keep :
Must thou rise ? thy Saviour rose
And has burst the prison door ;
All death's journey through HE knows,
HE has trod its path before.
Cease thy fear, Death has no sting,
And the Grave no triumphing ;
Come and see what radiance glows
Round the Tomb whence JESUS rose.

Christ is Risen.

FOR EASTER DAY.

"He is not here: for He is risen, ... Come, see the place where the Lord lay." S. MATT. xxviii. 6.

Hail, blest Morn, with glory bright,
Breaking on so dark a night !
Hail, blest Day, thy rising brings
Light and Life upon its wings :
Light it brings instead of gloom,
Life and triumph from the Tomb !
Hail, ye forms in dazzling white,
Come the happy news to tell,
Christ is risen in His might,
Christ has conquer'd Death and Hell ;—
　　　　　Christ has gained the victory !

Hark ! what earthquake shakes the ground !
Lo ! what brightness shines around !
See that huge stone roll'd away !
See those guards in dread dismay !
See those angel forms appear,
To the women drawing near !
These all tell the work is done,
JESU's pain and grief are o'er ;
He uprose before the Sun,
He hath burst the prison door :—
　　　　　Christ hath gained the victory !

Fear not ye, ye faithful few
Come the sepulchre to view ;
HE arose before the day,
Lo ! the place where JESUS lay !
See the linen thrown aside,
And the cloth His head that tied !
Linger not around the Grave,

Tarry not to seek Him here,
HE has risen, strong to save!
HE has risen, cease to fear!
    Christ has gained the victory!

Heav'n rejoice! Ye angels fly
Tell His triumph up on high!
Life's blest River, bear along
Joyous the exulting song!
Wave, ye palm-trees on its banks!
Bear it on, ye Cherub ranks!
Harpers, sweep the golden string,
Wake the hymn, the chorus swell;
Loud your alleluias sing,
Loud the raptur'd tidings tell :—
    Christ has gained the victory!

Christ has risen! Saints rejoice,
Lift, O lift, the happy voice!
HE is risen! and the stone,
Sealed and watched, is overthrown :
Christ has passed Death's portal through,
Op'ning Glory to the view!
Death is now a quiet Sleep,
No dread fears the Grave molest;
There the troubled cease to weep,
There the weary are at rest :—
    Christ has gained the victory!

Holy, humble men of heart,
In rejoicing bear your part!
Let your kindled hearts arise,
Up with JESUS to the skies :
He has gone in triumph there,
Heav'nly mansions to prepare :
HE for you this Day arose,
HE Who in such anguish died,
Light around the Grave He throws,
Glory's gates HE opens wide :—
    Christ has gained the victory!

Abide with us.

" But they constrained Him, saying, Abide with us : for it is
toward evening, and the day is far spent." S. LUKE xxiv. 29.

The sun behind grey Olivet
  Hung in the cloudless sky,
And the long shadows of the trees
  Marked that the Eve was nigh :
Two forms in Holy Converse talked
  With a mysterious One,
And reached the distant village gate
  As sunk the setting sun :
They paused ! But oh what burning thoughts
  Glow'd in each wond'ring breast,
As they that Holy One constrained
  To enter as their guest :

    " Day is far spent
      Kind stranger, tarry here ;
    Abide with us,
      Ev'ning is drawing near."

Oh ! thus when life is closing round,
  And sinks the setting sun ;
And the long shadows of the tomb
  Tell that the night comes on :
In holy converse may we talk,
  Our Lord and God with Thee ;
And reach the dim and shadow'd gate
  In Thy blest company :
There may our hearts within us burn
  With Thy sweet Presence nigh ;
And Faith and pious longings breathe
  In holy ecstasy :—

    " Day is far spent,
      Kind Saviour, tarry here ;
    Abide with us,
      Ev'ning is drawing near ! "

XXXV.

THE

Christian's Rest.

Translated from the "CIRCA EXEQUIAS DEFUNCTORUM" of PRUDENTIUS.

FOR TUESDAY IN EASTER WEEK.

" They rest from their labours." REV. xiv. 13.

The hour will come, the hour will quickly come,
When the warm life with quick'ning impulse swelling
   Shall join its kindred dust; and re-assume
      Its former dwelling!

The lifeless form, erewhile amid decay
In cold Corruption's dreary chambers lying,
   Shall with its eager spirit wing away,
      To bright realms flying.

For this we freely shed the pious tear;
For this we load the corse with fond endearments;
   For this we place it on the fun'ral-bier
      In costly cerements.

We lay it down with love's unthought expense,
Wrapt in its snow-white shroud all pure and meetly,
   And spices with embalming frankincense
      Preserve it sweetly.

For this the rock is hollow'd out with care,
For this the tomb is held in sacred keeping,—
   Faith counts the cherish'd dust reposing there,
      Not dead—but sleeping!

xxxvi.

Restrain your grief, change each complaining breath,
Ye mothers, stay your tearful lamentation ;
These pledges are not lost; Life owns this death
Its reparation !

Now take, O earth, take him to thy calm breast,
There may he sleep from earthly toils reposing;
These relics we commit for peace and rest
To thy disposing !

Guard thou this body which we here consign,
For HE will come, to whom it is related,
And claim His own,—for in His form divine
It was created !

But while the body, crumbling in decay,
Shall wait its call from God to re-awaken,
Where shall the unhoused spirit flee away ?
To what realms taken ?

A way is open to the faithful soul,
A way of light to Paradise ascending,
A happy Land,—the wearied spirit's goal,—
Joy never ending !

There, grant Thy servant, O our Saviour dear,
Rest in that Country, free from sin and danger ;
Rest he could find not while he lingered here
An exiled stranger !

We twine the wreath, the violet we strew,
Where the dear bones await their resurrection ;
And the cold stone with odors sweet bedew
In fond affection !

Lo! I am with you always.

FOR THE END OF THE GREAT FORTY DAYS.

Lo! I AM WITH YOU! Though the op'ning skies
Receive me up before your wond'ring eyes:
Though seen no more in open presence near,
Still I am with you; still your cry will hear:
Oft you shall feel My unseen Spirit steal
Into your souls, and holy thoughts reveal:
Oft shall My Peace upon your hearts descend,
And Grace sufficient for each Trial lend.

Lo! I AM WITH YOU! Though a dark day come
And you are call'd to pain and martyrdom:
In persecution, in the dungeon drear,
Still I am with you, still to succour near;
In famine, in fatigue, in sore distress,
In awful vigils, in the wilderness
My Hand shall save you; though in perils toss'd,
Nothing can harm you; not a hair be lost!

Lo! I AM WITH YOU! When your prayer ascends
My eye beholds, My list'ning ear attends;
Where two or three are gathered I am nigh
To soothe your sorrows, and to change each sigh:
When you are met in love the Bread to break,
And drink the cup of Blessing for My sake,
Then I am very near, your souls to feed,
With inward nourishment and drink indeed.

Lo! I AM WITH YOU! In each age and time,
In ev'ry lot, in ev'ry change and clime;
The load to lighten, and the tear to dry,
In doubt and pain and sickness I am nigh:
To earth's Bethesda pool I healing bring
Touched with the pain of human suffering:
When death approaches and dark shades descend,
Lo! I am with you always to the end.

The Fields
White to the Harvest.

FOR WHITSUN-TIDE.

"There shall be an heap of corn in the earth, high upon the hills: his fruit shall shake like Libanus, and shall be green in the city, like grass upon the earth. PSALM lxxii. 16.

See! the world's wide Harvest field,
 White with its full ears is bending;
East and West their promise yield,
 Each the harvest-cry is sending:
"Come, the earnest work begin,
"Come, and reap Christ's harvest in!"

Now the "heap of corn," foretold,
 Waves on high upon the mountain:
Thick as Libanus of old,
 Rich as grass by Silo's fountain:
Rustling in the breeze it stands
Waiting for the reapers' hands!

White the fields on Southern Isles,—
 White on India's plains appearing,—
White the Greenland harvest smiles,
 White is many a Western clearing:
Far and near and left and right,
Lo! the harvest-field is white!

Forth, ye reapers, forth to toil!
 See the ready crops are waving:
Forth! for many a laden soil
 Faithful hand and heart is craving:
Fear ye not the tares of sin,
Reap the Lord's ripe harvest in!

Go and sow: and go and reap:
 Signs of life true hearts are testing;
Linger not, to faint and weep,
 This is not the time for resting:
"Welcome home," when Christ appears
Shall repay our toils and tears!

xxxix.

Peace, be still.

Learn, my heart, learn self-denial,
  Bear thy cross with patient will;
Sink not, shrink not, at thy trial,
  Jesus whispers:—peace, be still!

Ask not that thy cross be lighter,—
  Less abrupt Grief's dreary hill,—
Pray not that thy way be brighter,—
  Jesus whispers:—peace, be still!

Let not gloomy fears and sorrow
  With dark forms thy spirit fill;
Care not, dread not, for to-morrow,
  Jesus whispers:—peace, be still!

Sink not down in weary anguish,
  Droop not 'neath thy load of ill;
Struggle on, forbear to languish,
  Jesus whispers:—peace, be still!

Fear not, in Life's rude commotion,
  Sudden change, or tempest shrill;
Walking on the troubled ocean,
  Jesus whispers:—peace, be still!

When "the flesh is weak," and quaileth,
  When the heart grows faint and still,
Even then, as Nature faileth,
  Jesus whispers:—peace, be still!

xl.

THE GLORY OF THE CROSS.

Warrior of Christ, who oft when beaten down
Art cheer'd with light which scatters all thy fear ;
Who o'er the Cross seest the glitt'ring Crown,
And in each conflict, conquest waiting near :

> *It is the Glory of the Cross,*
> *Gaze on that glory, gaze ;*
> *Till its bright prize beyond the skies*
> *Fills thee with endless praise !*

Victor through Christ, who oft hast overcome
The world, temptation, and thine heart within,
And borne a secret, silent Martyrdom
In crucifying self and conqu'ring sin :

> *See, See the Glory of the Cross*
> *Awaits thy conquest won ;*
> *Keep it in sight, lose not its light,*
> *Till all thy fight is done.*

Herald of Christ, who bearest on the light,
Like Dayspring cheering many an heathen Isle,
And canst not deem what power, what word of might
Melts those wild hearts, and makes the desert smile :

> *It is the Glory of the Cross,*
> *The love of Him who died ;*
> *Whose sound must roll, till pole to pole*
> *Confess the Crucified.*

Ye Saints of Christ, who near the sapphire throne
Shall gaze on God, entranced in bliss profound ;
To whose clear sight each glory shall be shown,
To whose rapt ears be borne each blissful sound :—

> *Then shall the Triumph of the Cross*
> *From harps unnumbered swell ;*
> *When Christ shall see His Victory,*
> *And with His ransom'd dwell !*

PERRY, PRINTER, SIDMOUTH.